Who ate all the pies?

RaW
BBC

How to use this book

Enjoy reading this book together with a child. You don't have to read it all in one go. Find a relaxed time and somewhere you can be comfortable. If you have time, you could read it by yourself first. If you just look at the pictures and read the speech bubbles these will tell you the main events in the story.

When you are sharing the book, you could read the main story text. Help the child to join in.

- Ask them to read the text in the speech bubbles if they are starting to read.
- Encourage them to talk about details in the pictures.
- Guess what might happen next before you turn the page.
- Talk about the questions at the end of the page.

Above all, just enjoy sharing the story together.

Help with reading aloud

- If you have time, try reading the book by yourself first. Practise reading it out loud.
- You may not know all the words, but don't worry. If you are not sure how to say a word, split it up into parts and sound it out, e.g. comfortable would be com-for-ta-ble.
- If you are not sure what a word means, look at the pictures to see if there are any clues that may help.
- Some of the names are made up for the Amazing Travelling Space Circus. Look at the pages at the front of the book which show all the characters.

Next step

If you would like to find more help with reading, there are BBC RaW book groups all round the country. Call 0800 0150 950 to find your nearest RaW centre and to get some free advice on what to do next. Or visit our website (bbc.co.uk/raw) and enter your postcode to find your nearest RaW centre.

Published by the BBC
201 Wood Lane
London W12 7TS

© BBC 2007
All rights reserved.
Reproduction in whole or in part
prohibited without permission.

ISBN 978-1-86000-237-3

Written by Heather Morris

Illustrated by Peter Lawson

Characters created by
Firedog Design

Designed by Starfish Design,
Editorial and Project
Management Ltd

Printed in Great Britain by ESP
Colour Ltd

Printed on paper manufactured
from sustainable forests

In this book you will meet ...

Bamrod
the Blender

Bamrod is the scientist and maker of potions which very rarely work. Most people are too wise to try his potions, but once or twice Bamrod gets it right!

Socks
Bamrod's dog

Socks is a very friendly dog, but not very clever. Living with Bamrod has mixed-up the few brain cells she had.

Guv
the Ringmaster

Always busy running the circus – he's loved by everyone. He's quite old and needs his aerial soapbox to get around.

Mrs. Spectacles

The Ringmaster's wife, she runs the circus. She's a clever old woman who plans everything and looks after everyone.

Mr. Scatterbrain
the Clown

He loves to entertain people and make them laugh. He rides a jet-powered unicorn.

Thud
the Shooting Starr

Thud is very forgetful. He loves being shot out of his cannon, but he can't always find it.

Tiny
the Strongoid

A tiny girl who loves to play. She's pretty but so strong she often breaks things. The earth shakes when she skips.

Max

Max is Lara's elder brother. He is quite creative and has a good sense of humour. He enjoys spending time with Lara.

Lara

Lara is Max's younger sister. She really likes Max and feels safe with him. She is good company and very brave.

Kooloo
the Space Hamster

He loves eating biscuits and secretly would like to have his own spaceship. He can be very useful to Max and Lara.

Major Crash
and The Jet Pack Acrobats

A dance group who perform flying dances. Sometimes they bump into each other.

Bamrod the Blender has been working on a new magic potion for ages. He wants to take over the Amazing Travelling Space Circus. He is working on a potion that will transform Guv and Mrs. Spectacles into mice. Guv and Mrs. Spectacles run the circus.

The last potion Bamrod made turned his dog Socks into a cat which made her very cross indeed. But now Bamrod thinks he has got it right at last.

Bamrod needs to test his new potion. He takes a small glassful and tries to get people to drink it.

He offers it to Mr. Scatterbrain the Clown, 'Try this, it will make you funnier.' But Mr. Scatterbrain says, 'I may be daft, but I'm not that stupid.'

Bamrod offers it to Thud the Shooting Star, 'Try this, it will make you fly further.'

'I've got enough troubles without your potions,' Thud grumbles.

Finally, he tries Tiny the amazing Strongoid, 'Try this, it will make you stronger.' She just laughs, 'I'm strong enough already, thank you.' And she bends a lamp-post in half with her bare hands.

They all know Bamrod and his tricks and aren't going to fall for this one.

Bamrod is fed up. He knows his potion is nearly right, but he has to test it on someone. He goes back to his lab. Socks jumps up wagging her tail. She is a very friendly dog, but not a very clever one. Living with Bamrod has mixed-up the few brain cells she once had.

Bamrod sees her and decides to test the potion on Socks. He gives her some biscuits and pours the potion on top. She runs up and eats it eagerly.

Bamrod watches closely. A mouse is also watching, but Bamrod doesn't see it.

Socks finishes the biscuits and sneezes loudly. She feels very odd. She shakes her head and wags her tail. As she wags her tail, it grows longer and longer. Then her ears change shape. Her legs grow shorter. Her nose turns to a point. Finally she shrinks down to the size of a mouse.

Bamrod does a little dance of delight. He believes his potion works.

Socks and the mouse stare at each other. They look exactly the same.

Do you think Bamrod's potion has worked?

Now Bamrod knows his potion works. He also knows that he won't be able to make Guv and Mrs. Spectacles drink it. He decides to hide the potion in some tasty pies. He adds a secret spice to make them smell really good. He sets to work and bakes a big pile. He leaves them to cool by the window.

Max and Lara walk past with Kooloo the space hamster. They can smell something tasty and then they see the pies on the windowsill. There is nobody in sight, so Max and Lara each take one. Kooloo bounces up and down squeaking loudly. They both look up at him as they bite into the pies.

At once Lara starts to feel very odd. Her skin is all itchy. It starts to grow fur. Her nose twitches. Her arms and legs grow shorter. Her fingernails turn into claws. Max feels just as odd. Suddenly they both shrink down to the size of a hamster.

Max and Lara and Kooloo stare at each other. They all look exactly the same.

 Do you think Max and Lara should have eaten the pies?

The Jet Pack Acrobats have been trying some new dance moves. They are not very good but have finally got them right. They hardly bump into each other at all now. This has made them very hungry. They can smell the tasty pies. They can't resist and they each take one.

There is complete confusion as they all change into each other. They suddenly

start bumping into each other and falling about. They have no idea what has happened to them. Major Crash arrives. The Acrobats all look exactly the same to him, but they are behaving very strangely. He has no idea what has happened.

What do you think has happened to the Acrobats?

Bamrod returns. He sees that all the pies have gone, except two. He is very cross as his plan has nearly been ruined. He grabs the last two pies and rushes off to the circus.

Guv and Mrs. Spectacles are just sitting down for a nice cup of tea. They have a plate of cakes to share. Bamrod hides behind the tent flap. He slips his two pies onto the plate. Guv and Mrs.

Spectacles take one each, without really looking. Bamrod is so excited that he pops out from behind the tent. Guv and Mrs. Spectacles both stare at him in surprise as they bite into the pies.

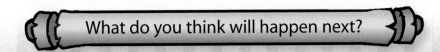
What do you think will happen next?

It's too late. Guv and Mrs. Spectacles both turn into copies of Bamrod. Max, Lara and Kooloo rush into the tent. They stare at the three Bamrods and realise what has happened. When anyone eats one of Bamrod's pies they turn into the person they are looking at.

The problem is – what to do now? How can they get Guv and Mrs. Spectacles back? They don't even know which is the right Bamrod to ask.

Back at Bamrod's house, Socks and the mouse have been getting on well. They have been nibbling through the boxes, packets and potions in Bamrod's lab.

Socks is sniffing at a test tube with a bright green liquid. It is an early version of the new potion. She licks up a little and starts to feel very odd again.

She twitches her tail and it grows shorter and shorter. Then her ears change shape. Her legs grow longer. Her nose is round again. Finally she grows back to the size of a dog. The old Socks appears again. She is very excited.

Lara, Max and Kooloo burst in. They are determined to find the cure for Bamrod's potion. They look at the mess in the lab. They see the nibbled packets and spilt test tubes. Socks jumps up and barks loudly. Max pats her on the head.

'Where shall we start?' he groans. Socks jumps higher and barks more loudly.

Max and Lara sit down gloomily. But Kooloo is listening hard to Socks. Socks pushes Kooloo towards the test tube with the green liquid. Kooloo realises

what she is trying to tell them. They both drag Max and Lara over. They stare at the test tube. They look at Socks and Kooloo who are both very excited now.

Lara asks, 'What are you trying to tell us?' Socks and Kooloo jump up and down wildly. Lara and Max look at each other. They both speak together, 'I wonder if…' 'Will this help?'

'Well, I'll try it if you do,' Lara decides. So they both take a sip of the green liquid. An instant later Max and Lara are standing there back in their proper shapes.

Max, Lara, Kooloo and Socks set off back to the circus carrying the test tube very carefully. On the way they meet Major Crash. He is sitting with his head in his hands. The Jet Pack Acrobats are still falling about and crashing in to each other.

'I just don't know what's happened to them,' the Major says. 'They were very good at the new dance moves but now look at them! They don't know if they are coming or going. It's a disaster!'

Max and Lara look at each other. 'I think we might be able to help,' Lara says.

They quickly explain about Bamrod's potion. Then they give each of the Acrobats a few drops of the green liquid. There is a moment of complete confusion. Then all the Acrobats stand up straight. They look just the same to Max and Lara, only now they are not falling over and bumping into each other.

Major Crash looks very relieved and he thanks Max and Lara. 'Fall in men,' he shouts. There is a moment's pause, then the Acrobats all line up and whizz off without bumping into each other!

Max and Lara arrive at the circus with the last few drops of the green liquid. The three Bamrods are arguing. Max and Lara look at them. They can't tell which is the real Bamrod.

'Who shall we give it to?' asks Max.

'What if we choose the wrong one?' worries Lara.

'We're just going to have to take a chance,' decides Max. He chooses the Bamrod who is shouting the loudest and gives him the potion.

Does Max get it right?

Just then Socks bounces into the tent. She looks at the two Bamrods and for a moment is puzzled. Then she leaps over to one of them and starts licking his hand.

'I think that's answered the question,' says Lara and gives the last few drops to the other Bamrod. Sure enough, Guv reappears.

The real Bamrod realises it is all over and storms out of the tent. Socks runs after him wagging her tail hard. She has no idea what's been happening.

'Well, after all that excitement I think we need some tea and proper pies all round,' says Mrs. Spectacles.